First Rite

by John Cole
Illustrated by Mary Beth Owens

Down East Books
Camden, Maine

Text copyright © 2004 by John Cole. All rights reserved.
Illustrations copyright © 2004 by Mary Beth Owens. All rights reserved.

Design by Lindy Gifford

Printed in China

5 4 3 2 1

ISBN 0-89272-621-0

Library of Congress Control Number 2004110914

Down East Books
P.O. Box 679
Camden, ME 04843

A division of Down East Enterprise, publishers of *Down East* magazine,
www.downeast.com

To request a book catalog or place an order, visit www.downeastbooks.com,
or call 800-685-7962.

It is snowing, and I wonder if I am too late. Here in these Maine woods of pine and balsam, the snow is gentled by the salt sea just beyond the ridge. Its fluid, heaving presence still holds something of August's warmth even in this late December. A southeast breeze off the water nudges the tops of the tallest pines, clots the snow with its briny fragrance. The flakes swell, become pale feathers so saturated with the nearby sea that they caress my cheeks with the gentle wetness of a summer rain.

It is four days before Christmas, and I have come to take our tree. For me it is an annual rite that reaches across decades to Christmases past, when, as a boy, I found purpose in the responsibility. Then it was city streets I roamed late on Christmas Eve as tree sellers hunched over their trash-can fires, pulled their overcoats closer, and hoped for stragglers to buy the trees that leaned so incongruously against stone skyscrapers. Racing through those dark and solemn streets, I would find the best of those trees and trot home, tugging my prize, then run breathless up the stairs to the room where those city trees always stood.

That boy within has survived the decades. He is still here every Christmas, still stirred by the annual adventure. On this late, lowering afternoon, amid its soft cascade of soggy snow, I wonder if both man and boy have overreached their grasp. But I am not afraid. These woods I know. They are my woods now. Our home, with yet another generation of Christmas young, lies at the sea's edge, over the rise.

I can find my way there even on a moonless midnight. It is the tree that troubles me now. In this snow, this early December dusk, will I be able to find the perfection that the proud boy within me demands? There is a houseful of critics waiting to comment on the tree's conformation, taper, and fullness of bough, on the perfection of its topmost spire, poised for crowning with our crystal star.

So I press my search, meeting ghosts in the snow that slides silent among the evergreens. These woods are easily walked. Its fourth- and fifth-generation trees sprout in scattered patches—spindly replicas of the giants that once marched across this land to the very brink of the granite-rimmed bay.

The pure and massive titans that once embraced every cove gave this place its colonial purpose. With axe and saw the Yankees of three centuries past toppled every tree, towed it over the ridge to the water's edge. There, with the spirit of Euclid at their side, they fashioned the finest wooden sailing ships the world had ever seen. Those great ships sailed 'round the Horn to China and beyond from the very cove our home now overlooks, the place where, at the lowest tides, the timbered skeletons of launching ways lie at eternal rest.

In their wake, those Yankee fleets left the rubble
of virgin forest. These woods where I stand were
riverbeds of stumps, their mammoth presence the
only memorial to the sacrificed majesty of the trees.
Soon even the stumps were gone, yanked by a second

Yankee generation, determined to create hayfields
where forests had been, barns where birches had
soared. For yet another century those farms pros-
pered; then, like the wooden ships gone aground,
they withered, shrank, rotted, and finally vanished.

Where I stand was once pasture, the hard land plowed by an Orr, a Pennell, a Simpson, or a Spinney: the shipbuilders' grandsons. Now *their* sons are lawyers, engineers, and merchants. I stand in these woods with the blue-eyed ghosts of their forebears, woods where the track of moose, the hoofprint of deer, and the tracery of partridge still mark the snow.

The wild creatures returned as pasture pine took over and the last of the cordwood cutters stripped the third-generation woodlot, leaving slash and brush piles to shelter the cottontail rabbit and snowshoe hare, new growth to feed the porcupine, and thickets enough to hide deer and give moose safe shelter, all just five miles from town.

With them, I am one of this century's tenants, arrived to share it with these creatures, to live lightly upon it, and to come, as I have this dark December afternoon, for the taking of the Christmas tree.

As I walk with snow-silenced footsteps, the
settlers, shipbuilders, and saltwater farmers of
yesteryear stride alongside me, axes in hand, just
as they must have in their Decembers, each looking
for his yuletide tree. Of all the nation's holiday

symbols, this is the longest-lasting, the most persis-
tently renewed, whether by a boy running a city's
Christmas streets or a man-boy alone in the Maine
woods, hearing voices in the sighing pines.

I must hesitate no longer, or surely night will arrive and I shall walk, treeless, down the woods path and along the snowy country road that takes me home.

Here. Is this the tree? This thick-framed balsam, vigorous, well-sinewed in comparison to its neighbors? It is tall enough, perhaps too tall, and we shall need to mar the top's fine symmetry to raise it again indoors. I am having difficulty judging such matters in the thickening dusk and billowing snow.

I silence all doubts: This is the tree.

Kneeling in the snow, my bucksaw held in front, I feel the balsam's lowest boughs press my shoulders. They tremble a bit as the saw bites and the fragrance of fir mixes with the soft sea wind. I am in a small, wild universe now, the boughs on my back, the snow-covered ground beneath my knees, and the darkness of the small December world between the tree and the ground where I kneel. My eyes hold on the trunk of the fir as the resin's perfume grows with each labored stroke of the saw.

Then my work is done.

The tree eases over but does not fall. Its boughs are too thick, too close to the earth. They cushion the fall of the fir so it reclines with dignity, a monarch going gracefully to rest.

I rise, fit the saw over my shoulder, and grip the base of the tree's lowest bough. As I walk with the balsam in tow, sliding easily across the snow, the woods fold in behind me, keeping their ghosts and creatures.

The hour is not yet four, but I find it difficult to see the trail, so swiftly does the afternoon become evening. This, I tell myself, must be the year's shortest day, and in that moment I find more than mere understanding of the gloom.

It is, I realize, in the time of the winter solstice—
indeed, the very hour when the sun will dip to the
lowest point of its lowest arc in these heavens. There
it will pause, shuddering with the enormity of its celes-
tial shift, and then, with movement majestic, infini-
tesimal, it will begin the pattern of ascendancy that
will carry it to the zenith of our summer skies in June.

Instead of dusk about me I see beyond the
horizon, to the core of that invisible sun, the great

star that is at this moment repeating the rituals of
thousands of millions of solstice beginnings. What I
am witnessing here in these woods—and what millions and millions of us share in our northern hemi-
sphere at Christmas week—is something more than
winter's beginning. It is an annual solar journey that
speaks to us of renewal, of the restoration of light, of
earlier dawns, longer twilights, more brilliant days.
Until at last spring blossoms and summer blooms.

Beyond those who felled the virgin forests; beyond even the ancient tribes who walked the land before them; beyond the shipbuilders, farmers, merchants, and engineers; beyond the life of these woods and the streets of the cities; beyond me and my family's span, the sun moves in the heavens. And on this December evening, four days before Christmas, this greatest of stars turns to start the journey that will take it to the center of our skies.

There is a gift in this natural event as inspiring as any Christmas ritual. Knowing that the solstice proceeds even as I labor along our home road, I am filled with joy at the task that the boy in me has completed on this December afternoon, in these Maine woods.

I can see our porch lights now. I am up the steps, opening the front door, surging into the room with the tree following. As the fir squeezes through the door, its boughs compress, then spring back, flinging snow, ice, and crystal droplets across the floor like a wild thing captured. This tree is alive, like a colt. It shakes, trembles, fills our Christmas house with its vital wildness.

In a while, it is tamed and stood upright where it will stand through all the days of Christmas. Until another December, the first rite is done.